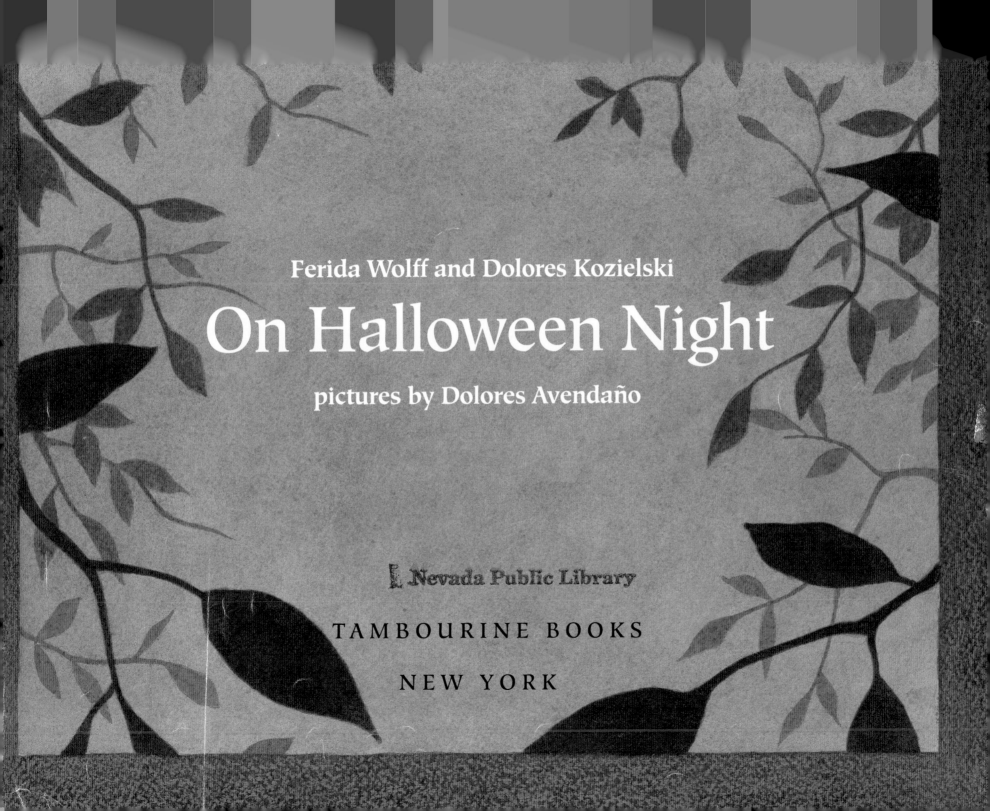

Ferida Wolff and Dolores Kozielski

On Halloween Night

pictures by Dolores Avendaño

TAMBOURINE BOOKS

NEW YORK

Library of Congress Cataloging in Publication Data   Wolff, Ferida, 1946-
On Halloween night/by Ferida Wolff and Dolores Kozielski; illustrated
by Dolores Avendaño. — 1st ed. p. cm.   Summary: Thirteen suitably
creepy things from witches to snakes and ghosts are counted in
honor of Halloween. [1. Halloween—Fiction. 2. Counting.
3. Stories in rhyme.] I. Kozielski, Dolores. II. Avendaño,
Dolores, ill. III. Title. PZ8.3.W844On 1994 [E]—dc20
93-26859 CIP AC ISBN 0-688-12972-2 (TR). —
ISBN 0-688-12973-0 (LE)
10 9 8 7 6 5 4 3 2 1
First edition

For Leahe, with love   F.W.

To my parents, Mary and Charles Cirillo   D.K.

To my mother and father, with love   D.A.

One witch stirs
up a bubbling pot,
adding this, adding that,
mixing such a tasty brew,
on Halloween night.

Oo-oo-oo-ooh.

Two cats claw
in a garbage can,
tossing this, tossing that,
digging till the morning dew,
on Halloween night.
Oo-oo-oo-ooh.

Three owls hunt
through the frosty mist,
grabbing this, grabbing that,
hooting at each startled shrew,
on Halloween night.
Oo-oo-oo-ooh.

Four goats butt
round the rattling shed,
crashing this, crashing that,
banging barn boards painted blue,
on Halloween night.
Oo-oo-oo-ooh.

Five snakes slink
over autumn leaves,
rustling this, rustling that,
sliding through an old, worn shoe,
on Halloween night.
Oo-oo-oo-ooh.

Six bears tramp
through the haunted woods,
stomping this, stomping that,
growling at the caribou,
on Halloween night.
Oo-oo-oo-ooh.

Seven wolves prowl
for a midnight meal,
stalking this, stalking that,
howling in the full moon's view,
on Halloween night.
Oo-oo-oo-ooh.

Eight toads croak
in the shivery swamp,
warning this, warning that,
hiding from a close canoe,
on Halloween night.
Oo-oo-oo-ooh.

Nine crows dance
in the pumpkin field,
flapping this, flapping that,
stamping out a tune—one, two,
on Halloween night.
Oo-oo-oo-ooh.

Ten hares hop
through the old, dried stalks,
sniffing this, sniffing that,
seeking fallen corn to chew,
on Halloween night.
Oo-oo-oo-ooh.

Eleven bats swoop
from a musty cave,
shrieking this, shrieking that,
settling in a chimney flue,
on Halloween night.
Oo-oo-oo-ooh.

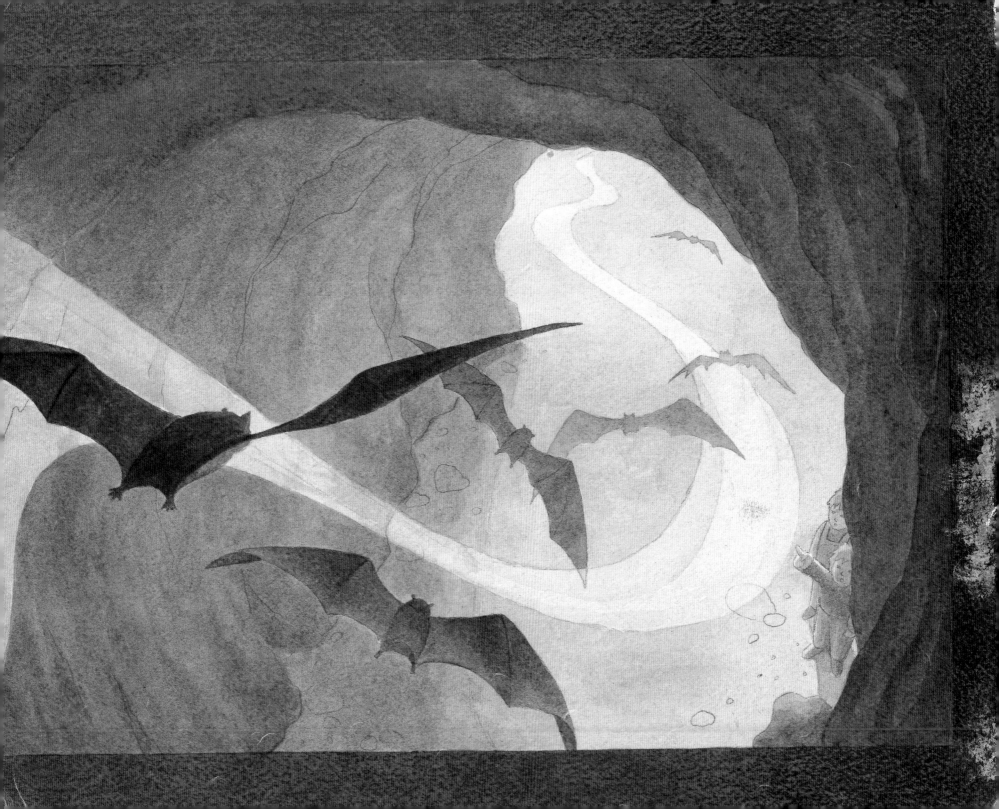

Twelve bugs creep
in a crooked house,
grubbing this, grubbing that,
feeding on cold, dried-up stew,
on Halloween night.
Oo-oo-oo-ooh.

Thirteen ghosts haunt
at the old school yard,
climbing this, climbing that,
zooming down the slide toward you,
on Halloween night.

BOOOOOO!